Dezbah

and the

Dancing Tumbleweeds

---

by

Margaret Kahn Garaway

Illustrations by

Cathie Lowmiller

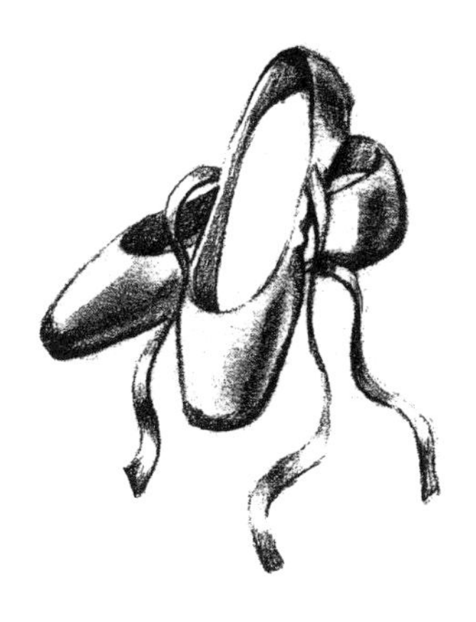

Old Hogan Publishing Company

Published By
Old Hogan Publishing Company
P.O. Box 91978
Tucson, Arizona 85752-1978

Other Books by Margaret Kahn Garaway

Ashkii and His Grandfather
in English/
English and Spanish
The Old Hogan
The Old Hogan Coloring Book
The Teddy Bear Number Book
in English and Spanish

Third Printing 1996

Library of Congress Catalog Card Number 94-69385

ISBN 0-9638851-2-X

Printed by Sahuaro Press, Ltd., 700 North Stone Avenue,
Tucson, Arizona 85705

To my husband, who has
supported me in all my endeavors.

M.K.G.

1

Dezbah ran with the grace of a deer across the desert, shouting, "Wait for me, wait for me!" The slender Navajo girl was trying to catch up with her older sister and brother who were now within hearing distance.

Dezbah's sister, Mariana, an eighth grader, was the star runner on the junior high track team. She had set a new district-wide record in her division for the 100-meter dash. Dezbah thought that Mariana was the greatest! She wanted more that anything else in the world to be an outstanding runner like her sister. She also had a secret dream of becoming the first Navajo girl to win a medal for the U.S. Olympic women's track team. She could hardly wait to go to junior high next year and be on the school track team.

Jimmy, Dezbah's brother and a seventh grader, was one of the top runners on the boys' team. All through the summer the three had worked out on their homemade track every morning before the sun began to bake the desert floor. They continued running laps each morning even though school had started. "Come on Dezbah, it's time to go to school," Jimmy had called to his sister as he and Mariana were leaving the track.

"Just a few minutes. I'll catch up with you," Dezbah had responded. She was enjoying her own effortless breathing and the feeling of her feet barely touching the earth beneath her. She didn't want to stop just yet.

Although reluctant to leave the track, Dezbah took off in high spirits, thinking of the great workout she had that morning. She ran in quick, smooth strides, leaping easily over any sagebrush in her path. The sun was rising above the horizon as a flock of small birds flew out of a clump of brush and burst up before her. She put forth a spurt of speed as she drew closer to Mariana and Jimmy, calling out to them again.

The two on the other side of the highway stopped at their sister's call. They turned just in time to see a pickup truck moving down the road as Dezbah was about to cross.

"A truck! Wait, don't . . ." yelled Mariana.

Dezbah did not hear her sister. Her only thought was to catch up with Jimmy and Mariana.

The truck screeched to a stop. Mariana and Jimmy stood frozen to the ground. They saw the driver leap out of the truck and run to the other side but they could not see Dezbah.

They ran to the pickup truck. Dezbah lay motionless in the sagebrush alongside the road. The driver, an Anglo man, was checking the unconscious girl's pulse and listening to her heart. The shaken bilagáana said, "I think she'll be O.K. but we'll have to get her to a hospital. She can't be moved until the ambulance arrives. I'm sorry. It all happened so fast."

A car stopped and a man called out, "Do you need any help?"

"Yes!" the driver of the pickup replied. "Please go to the school and have them call an ambulance!"

Mariana and Jimmy stood there frightened and helpless. Mariana finally said to Jimmy, "I'll wait here for the ambulance and go to the hospital with Dezbah. You run home and tell Mom and Dad what has happened. Maybe Auntie can take them to the hospital."

It didn't take long for the ambulance to arrive. Mariana sat beside her sister, struggling to hold back her tears as they were rushed to the hospital. Her fingernails dug into the palms of her hands while she watched Dezbah slip in and out of consciousness. When they arrived at the hospital Mariana reluctantly went into the waiting room when the doctor took her sister into the examining room.

Dezbah's parents arrived just as the doctor was finished with the examination. The doctor approached the huddled group and said, "Dezbah will be fine, but we will have to keep her in the hospital about a week. She is suffering from a slight concussion besides the bruises on her body. She is also in shock and will need lots of bed rest. We have ordered x-rays to see if she has broken any bones."

"When can we see her?" asked her father.

"She's in x-ray now. When she's back in her room the nurse will come for you," the doctor answered. "You will be able to see her but she'll probably be asleep. She has gone through a terrible experience."

An hour later the family sat in silence by Dezbah's bed, unable to help, but not wanting to leave her. The girl's eyes were closed as she lay still and distant from them. She was suspended between consciousness and sleep, thinking faraway thoughts.

In a dreamy mist Dezbah remembered her joyous morning, but she was aware that something bad had happened to her. Her body was floating somewhere nearby, yet it wasn't her body. *My legs are so far away! They'll never carry me like the wind again.* She drifted away into nothingness.

The doctor opened the door and motioned the family out into the hall. "We have the results of the x-rays," he said. "Dezbah has broken her left arm. We'll have to put it in a cast. No other bones are broken. She's lucky she fell into the sagebrush. There is no need for you to remain. We'll take good care of her. You may see her whenever you can. Since you live so far away, you may not be able to see her during the week. We'll let you know when to come to take her home."

Each day the doctor checked on Dezbah's progress. On the fifth day he said, "Dezbah, you're doing very well. It's time for you to get out of bed and walk. Nurse will help you. You may be a little dizzy from being in bed so long."

When the nurse offered to help, Dezbah could not lift her legs and swing them off the bed. They felt lifeless. The thing she feared the most was true — she couldn't walk. *I knew I couldn't!* Tears welled up, hidden, her throat closed, and she gave in to despair with a kind of grim, tragic resignation. *I knew, I knew,* she reminded herself.

The nurse sent for the doctor. They stood by the bed, puzzled. They could not understand what had gone wrong.

"Maybe there's a hairline fracture I overlooked," the doctor said to the nurse. After going over the x-rays very carefully he said, "I can't find the problem. I'll call in a bone specialist."

The bone doctor gave Dezbah a thorough examination and studied the x-rays, but she could find nothing that would keep Dezbah from using her legs. Dezbah overheard the two doctors discussing her, neither one able to determine the reason for the paralysis. When she heard them remark that they could find nothing physically wrong, that it was just a matter of time until she walked again, she became angry.

Bilagáana doctors can't know how I feel! My chance of being the first Navajo girl to win a medal in the Olympics is over! Grief and anger filled her throat and she found it hard to swallow.

From the time Dezbah had regained consciousness and recalled the accident, she was sure she would never walk or run again. The more she thought about it, the more convinced she became. She asked herself over and over again, *why me, why me?*

Dezbah shook herself out of her reverie and said to the doctors, "I know I won't ever walk again. I want to go home to my family."

Her doctor, realizing there was no convincing the girl at this time that she could walk, called in her parents to discuss the situation. "We see no reason why your daughter cannot walk," the doctor said when the parents arrived at the hospital. "Dezbah is convinced that she cannot walk. Until she believes that she can, she will not try. Perhaps if you have a Healing Ceremony the medicine man can help her. When the cast comes off her arm she'll be able to use crutches. Until then we'll give her a wheelchair. Come back with Dezbah in about four weeks."

2

When Dezbah and her parents arrived home from the hospital Jimmy went out to the car and brought in the wheelchair setting it down upon the hardpacked mud floor of the hogan. Father carried his daughter inside and placed her gently in the chair, while the family gathered around. Her parents were upset to see their daughter in this condition. She had been the most outgoing of their children — always bubbling with excitement, but now sitting subdued and dejected in the wheelchair.

Her younger brother and sister stared at her. They had not seen their sister since the day of the accident and did not understand what was going on.

Mariana and Jimmy started to fling questions at Dezbah. "What was it like in the hospital? What

kind of food did they give you? Did you like the food? Why can't you walk?"

"Mariana and Jimmy, stop asking so many questions. Don't you see your sister isn't feeling well," admonished their father.

"I don't mind, shizhe'e. I can try to answer them. The food was different. I missed shimá's fry bread and mutton stew. I missed all of you. But I don't know why I can't walk. I have no feeling in my legs. Maybe it will be better after the Healing Ceremony." she said, sighing.

While Dezbah was in the hospital, her parents had made arrangements with the medicine man to have a Healing Ceremony when she returned home.

"What are you going to do about school, Dezbah?" Jimmy asked.

"We'll tell your teacher you're home now. She'll know what to do," said Mariana.

The family was taken by surprise when Dezbah suddenly blurted out, "No more questions, too much talking." She was overcome by the confusing emotions she was feeling, but did not know how to share them with her family.

Her mother said, "Children, go outside. Your sister needs quiet."

Shortly after the children had gone out, their grandparents, aunts and uncles drove up to the clearing. They had come to welcome Dezbah home.

They crowded into the hogan bringing in food to share with the family.

Dezbah's grandfather sat down by the wheelchair and took his granddaughter's hand in his. "How are you, sitsoi?" Without waiting for an answer he continued, "No granddaughter of mine will live in a wheelchair! You come from a family of warriors. Soon you will be running as fast as the wind."

Dezbah smiled at her grandfather. "Shicheii, I am happy you came. I have been feeling angry at what happened to me. The bilagáana doctor said I can walk and run, but I can't. Maybe the medicine man will help me."

By the time all the other members of the family visited with Dezbah she was feeling tired again. Before long most of the food was eaten and the family left. With a sigh of relief Dezbah sat back in the wheelchair and closed her eyes.

"Shizhe'e, it is good to be with the family again," Dezbah said to her father when he carried her to bed.

Life around the hogan continued the way it always had been for the rest of the family. The older children went off to school for the day while the two younger ones went to pre-school for the morning. Dezbah's father herded sheep all day. Mother remained at home keeping busy with the daily chores. She felt helpless when she saw Dezbah sitting in the wheelchair. Each day had found no improvement in her condition. Planning a Healing Ceremony for the ailing child was all she could do at this time.

Although Navajos use the white man's medicine they also use their own cures, which take place at Healing Ceremonies conducted by medicine men. It would be almost two weeks before the ceremony could take place. Father made plans to slaughter a sheep for the mutton stew that would be served at the end of the ceremony. Mother got the rest of the supplies ready for the stew and fry bread.

Dezbah preferred quiet and did not mind being alone most of the day. For the first couple of days, at least, she seemed content to sit in her wheelchair in the doorway of the hogan and look out on the desert. *How peaceful it is,* she thought, watching her uncle's horses and cattle grazing in the distance. *How sweet the newborn lambs are, leaping about and nuzzling their mothers,* observed the girl, when her father brought the sheep close by the hogan. *I feel happy looking at all the beauty and yet I feel sad. What is going to become of me?* She closed her eyes, looking for an answer to her dilemma.

Thinking about her grandfather, whom she dearly loved, Dezbah recalled the wonderful stories he told his grandchildren every winter; the tales of coyotes, bears, frogs, mountain lions and other animals in Navajo legends.

Dezbah gazed up at the sky as she opened her eyes. Looking at the clouds gathering overhead, she noticed that one looked like the mischievous coyote, a favorite of all the children. *You funny coyote, where are you hurrying?* she wondered as the cloud raced across the sky. She watched the coyote-cloud until it was no more.

Dezbah's little brother and sister were playing nearby. "Come here," she called to them. They ran over, eager for their sister's attention. "Let's play a game. Look up at the sky and see if you can find a sheep in the clouds."

"There, there," they shouted, nodding their heads toward a sheep. Dezbah's brother was almost five years old and her sister was three going on four. They were learning English in pre-school and liked repeating new words. The three played the game until Dezbah grew tired.

"That was fun," Dezbah said. "We can play again tomorrow." She was glad she had found something to keep her busy for a while.

3

A few days after returning from the hospital, Dezbah asked her mother, "Do you need any help, shimá? I'm getting tired of sitting in this wheelchair. I feel sad. I want to be running again."

Her mother sighed as she answered her daughter, "Dezbah, your arm is in a cast. You cannot card the wool for my weaving. Rest and get well. Would you like to go out now?"

Once outside Dezbah settled back in her chair and tried to enjoy the quiet afternoon, but she was not alone for long. Shortly after her mother had gone inside, she saw a car approaching on the road. It stopped in the clearing not far from the hogan. A tall, slender, young woman stepped out of the car and walked up to her.

"You must be Dezbah," the woman said. "I'm Miss Anderson, your teacher until you return to school. You will be able to keep up with your classwork."

"Yes, I'm Dezbah, but I won't be returning to school," she answered, annoyed. She was used to being alone, and she resented this intruder.

Miss Anderson feeling the hostility coming from Dezbah smiled at her new pupil, and said, "I understand. You have reason to be angry with the world, Dezbah. But maybe, in time, we'll be friends. I'll come every afternoon and teach you the same things the children in your class are learning."

The teacher's gentle reply in response to her rudeness made Dezbah feel ashamed, but she wasn't too sure of Miss Anderson's offer of friendship. At school she had liked some of her Anglo teachers but could she trust this now bilagáana teacher? She hadn't been too happy with the bilagáana doctor. *But I can't share my feelings with my family because it makes them sad,* she thought. *It would be so nice to have a friend I can confide in, who would be understanding.*

Dezbah's mother came out to see who was talking to her daughter. The two younger children clung to her skirt as she stood in the doorway. "Shimá, this is Miss Anderson. She's going to be my new teacher."

Glancing shyly at the young woman, her mother said, "Yá'át'ééh."

"Hello," answered Miss Anderson.

Mother went back into the hogan, leaving the two to their work.

Miss Anderson handed Dezbah a book. "Please read page one for me," she requested.

Dezbah hesitated for a moment, then gave a shrug and to Miss Anderson's surprise, read fairly well. "That was very good," the teacher said. "I really think we can work as a team."

"Maybe," mumbled Dezbah.

At the end of the lesson Miss Anderson gave her some homework to do. "I'll be giving you homework every day since I only see you for two hours each time. Please have it ready for me when I come. I'll see you tomorrow," she said as she departed.

After glancing hastily at the homework Dezbah put it aside. She was tired and she wasn't in the mood to do any more work that day. When Mariana and Jimmy came home Dezbah said to them, "My teacher came today."

"Do you like her?" asked Mariana.

"I don't know," answered Dezbah. "She left me homework, but I don't know if I want to do it."

"You better do it," her brother said, as he left to help his father.

The next day Miss Anderson asked Dezbah for her homework.

"I didn't do it." she replied.

"Why didn't you do it?" her teacher asked.

"I don't know what I need it for. I'll never walk again," the girl replied sullenly.

"Many people live in wheelchairs their entire lives, but that doesn't mean they can't learn and do something for themselves. Besides, it's too soon to say you won't walk again. I understand there's going to be a Healing Ceremony for you. Don't give up hope. You can't let your anger keep you from learning."

By the end of the lesson Dezbah said to her teacher, "I've been thinking about what you said. Maybe I have been acting stupid. I'm still angry about the accident."

Dezbah was busy writing when Jimmy and Mariana got home from school. "Hey, sister, are you doing your homework?" Jimmy asked. "What happened? I thought you weren't going to do it."

"I changed my mind. I only hurt myself if I don't," she answered.

"Dezbah, do you like your teacher better now?" Mariana inquired.

"She's O.K. She seems to be a nice bilagáana," answered Dezbah.

When Miss Anderson arrived the next day Dezbah immediately handed her the homework. After looking it over briefly the teacher said, "Dezbah, I like what I see so far."

When Miss Anderson left Dezbah decided that she might get to like her bilagáana teacher after all!

Each day after lunch Dezbah sat outside eagerly waiting for Miss Anderson's car to appear on the road. She now looked forward to having something to do every day.

The teacher grew to appreciate her new pupil. In addition to being bright, Dezbah showed a great sensitivity and awareness of life around her. She was always asking questions which Miss Anderson tried to answer. The two often discussed many things besides schoolwork.

One day the sky was full of white, fluffy clouds and Dezbah decided to share her cloud game with her teacher. "Look at the clouds in the sky, Miss Anderson," Dezbah said. "Can you find a cloud that looks like an animal? I love to play this game. It keeps me from getting bored."

"I see a sheep," Miss Anderson cried out. "Can you find it?"

"Oh, that's too easy," said Dezbah. "So many clouds look like sheep. It's right over the mesa. I see a coyote. Can you find it?"

"I've been coming to the reservation for six months and I've never seen a coyote!" Miss Anderson said. "What do they look like? The pictures I've seen remind me of wolves. Am I right?"

Dezbah said, "Look at the cloud above you. That is a coyote. It looks like a wolf or a big dog. I know lots of coyote stories if you would like to hear them."

"I would love to hear them when we have time after your lessons," replied Miss Anderson.

Dezbah smiled. She looked forward to retelling the stories of her grandfather, sharing part of her rich Navajo heritage with this teacher who had become a friend.

4

During her daily trip to the reservation Miss Anderson thought about Dezbah. After spending the first few days at the hogan she had noticed there were only a few comic books for Dezbah to read. When home the children helped their parents with the chores or played outside. They had no time for reading.

The day after her discovery, Miss Anderson appeared at the hogan with an armful of books. "Dezbah, look what I've brought you," she said. "These books are for girls your age. I read them when I was twelve and enjoyed them. This isn't a school assignment, so you can feel free to read them or not."

Dezbah shrugged her shoulders not knowing how she felt about the idea. "I'll look at them when I have time," the girl said, putting the books on the chair beside her.

Nothing further was said about the books that afternoon. When Miss Anderson left all she said was, "I'll see you tomorrow, Dezbah."

When Jimmy and Mariana came home from school and saw the pile of books, they said, "Where did you get all those books, Dezbah?"

"Miss Anderson brought them today. She thought I'd like to read them," she answered.

Looking through the books the next morning, Dezbah decided to read the one that looked the easiest. She had always picked out the easy ones from the school library to read in the classroom. They couldn't take books home because too many kids forgot to bring them back. The book Dezbah chose was harder than the books she had been reading in school and found it more interesting. She enjoyed the story and the morning went faster than it had during the past week.

Dezbah was surprised that she hated to put the book down when Miss Anderson arrived that afternoon. "I see you like the book," Miss Anderson said.

"Oh yes, Miss Anderson, but I find that I don't know the meaning of some of the words. Sometimes I can guess what they mean and sometimes I can't."

"Don't worry about them. I want you to enjoy the story and if you look up each word it takes away

many of the
role of Odette-

the pleasure of reading. What you can do is write down each word but continue reading. Later you can look up the meaning. Do you have a dictionary?" her teacher asked.

When Dezbah shook her head, Miss Anderson said, "I'll bring you one tomorrow."

The lesson went well that afternoon but for the first time since Miss Anderson began teaching, Dezbah didn't mind when she left. The book was exciting and she wanted to get back to reading it.

Each afternoon after Miss Anderson left, Dezbah noticed that her little brother and sister kept staring at the book. "Little ones, would you like me to read you a story?" she asked them.

They nodded their heads. The teacher in preschool read to them, but no one had ever read to them at home. "I'll ask my teacher to bring some books for you," Dezbah said.

After the lessons the next day Dezbah said to her teacher, "Miss Anderson, could you bring some easy books I can read to my little brother and sister? They see me reading, and they're very curious."

"Of course, Dezbah. I'll get some easy picture books they can keep. You have no idea how happy this makes me."

"Dezbah," she continued, "I would like to start you on a music program, but before we begin, tell me what you know about music."

"All I know is Navajo music I hear at powwows, squaw dances, and other gatherings. I like country music that I hear on the Navajo radio station. I never thought about music. I mostly thought about playing and running," Dezbah replied.

"O.K.," Miss Anderson said. "I'll bring you a surprise tomorrow."

The following day Miss Anderson brought a portable cassette player and some tapes. "The music I brought you is very different from what you know. It is called orchestral music. We will listen to the different instruments of the orchestra and learn to recognize their sounds as well as learning to understand and appreciate the music. I also brought some country music tapes, since you like that music."

After she had listened to the music tapes for several days, Dezbah said to Miss Anderson, "Music makes me think of all the things I see around me. I hear the sound of storms, wind blowing through sagebrush, cries of birds flying and livestock moving around. Sometimes the music makes me feel happy and sometimes sad. Is that what music is supposed to do?"

"Music does different things for different people. I'm glad to see that it is doing something for you," Miss Anderson said. "I would like you to write down what you like and don't like about the music you are listening to. In a few days we'll discuss it.

"Miss Anderson, a few days ago I started reading *Little Women* by Louisa May Alcott. It's the hardest book I've ever read, but I like it," Dezbah said.

"Why do you find it hard and what do you like about it?" asked Miss Anderson.

"The author uses lots of new words, more words than I've ever seen before and it makes me think. The people talked different a long time ago. Sometimes I don't understand what they are saying. But I like reading about how people lived then. They wore different kinds of clothes, even different from the clothes I see bilagáana around here wearing. Their houses were different, too. I like reading about the four sisters. Each sister is so different. I like Jo the best. She isn't afraid to try new things. I wish I was as brave as she is."

"What you say is very interesting," said Miss Anderson. "I would like you to finish the book and then we can talk about it. When you finish the story you can decide if you still like Jo the best. If you have any questions while you're reading it, put them down on a piece of paper and I'll try to answer them. I wish I could stay longer, but I must leave now."

As soon as Miss Anderson drove away Dezbah picked up her book to read. She was engrossed in the story when Mariana and Jimmy came home from school.

The two had been noticing their sister reading every time they came home. Their curiosity was aroused.

"Do you really like the books, Dezbah? Aren't they hard to read?" Mariana asked her.

"Yeah, it must be hard!" echoed Jimmy.

"They're hard," answered Dezbah, "but the more I read the easier it gets. I was going to ask you if you want to read any. I'll be glad to share them with you. You can try an easier one first."

"Maybe one of these days I'll read one," Jimmy said, as they went into the hogan.

The days were going very fast for Dezbah. Between her schoolwork, reading, listening to music and reading to her brother and sister she had little time to worry about herself. She was able to wait patiently for the day of the Healing Ceremony.

5

Time was not going fast enough for Dezbah's parents who were very concerned about their daughter. Despite the pleasure the girl was deriving from all the new things she was learning, she was not sleeping well. Every night Dezbah cried out in her sleep, as though experiencing her accident over and over again. They were anxious for the Healing Ceremony to take place.

At last it was time for the ceremony. The night was cool and crisp. The stars shone brightly. Only car headlights broke through the darkness as friends and family arrived at the hogan. The people who had come to wish Dezbah well filled the one-room dwelling until there was not an inch of space to spare. The seriousness of the occasion could be felt throughout the large room.

Miss Anderson had been invited to attend the sing. This would be her first Healing Ceremony and she was full of curiosity and concern. Upon arrival the young teacher joined the other guests sitting on the dirt floor across the room from her pupil. Dezbah, with bowed head, sat alone upon a Pendleton blanket spread out on the floor. Miss Anderson wanted to go over to the girl and offer some encouraging words but it didn't look like it was the proper thing to do.

Dezbah was looking at all the people around her. *Have they come just to see me walk?* she wondered. *Maybe they ought to leave right now, because I know I'm going to disappoint them.* She felt torn by her desire to regain the use of her legs and the deep-seated fear that continued to haunt her — the fear that she would never walk or run again. She closed her eyes and tried to clear her mind of doubt and anxiety. She opened them as the ceremony began.

Everyone's attention was drawn to a small circle of family members chanting in rhythm to the beat of the sacred rattle the medicine man was shaking. A short time later he left the group and knelt down in front of Dezbah. The medicine man or singer as he is often called, chanted as he passed the small bundle of twigs, tied with a leather thong along the girl's bare legs and over her body. After sprinkling corn pollen over his patient he returned to the

circle of singers sitting not far from Dezbah. He would be going between Dezbah and the singers throughout the evening.

At one point in the ceremony Dezbah's mother invited Miss Anderson to join the singers. The young woman felt honored to be included. When the medicine man offered Miss Anderson the sacred rattle her eyes moistened. She knew she would never forget this night. Although she did not understand the Navajo words of the prayers, she was deeply touched and added her own silent prayer. When the singer went back to Dezbah, Miss Anderson returned to her place with the guests.

Each time the medicine man was with Dezbah he repeated the ceremony with the twigs, and each time Miss Anderson watched for some kind of reaction from Dezbah. Outwardly the girl seemed to remain passive, showing no emotion.

The medicine man sprinkled corn pollen on Dezbah at the conclusion of the ceremony after which everyone was served the food prepared by Dezbah's mother.

A few days after the ceremony, the medicine man came to see how Dezbah was doing. He found no change in her condition. "I am not surprised," he said to her parents. "I watched Dezbah very closely during the ceremony and I saw much fear in her face. Her mind was not ready to accept healing. We can have another ceremony for her in one month."

Her parents were disappointed when they heard those words but they had great faith in the medicine man and respect for his judgment.

Her father said, "We understand and appreciate your effort. We will let you know if it will be necessary."

The following day Dezbah's mother told Miss Anderson what the medicine man had said. "We are grateful that you are teaching our daughter. You have helped her very much. She is happy when you are here. Please keep coming to our hogan."

Miss Anderson nodded her head and took the older woman's hands gently in hers. She did not know what to say. She wished she had some encouraging words to offer the mother.

6

Miss Anderson would not see her favorite student until Monday. She was worried about Dezbah because she had shown no improvement after the Healing Ceremony. The girl needed something to give her new hope and encouragement the teacher kept thinking.

The next morning was Saturday and Miss Anderson sat reading the newspaper while relaxing at home after breakfast. Turning a page of the paper, she came upon an announcement of a touring ballet company coming to their town. *That's it! The very thing Dezbah needs!* thought Miss Anderson. *I'll get tickets and take her to see a live ballet.*

Miss Anderson loved everything about ballet and had shared this love with her special pupil. She had brought Dezbah her tapes of ballet music and books on the subject. Listening to the music every day and talking about the stories with her teacher, Dezbah also became fond of ballet. On Monday Miss Anderson went to the reservation, tickets in hand, hoping they would help Dezbah get through this latest setback.

As she got out of the car and approached Dezbah, her heart sank. Her student's eyes had always lit up with joy upon seeing her. But this time, the teacher was greeted only by a glum and sullen face.

Before she could speak, Dezbah cried out, "I didn't do my homework! You needn't have come today! What's the use of studying or doing anything? I'll never walk again!" She turned her head away, trying to control the tears brimming in her eyes.

Miss Anderson sat down on a stump in the clearing. She said nothing. When Dezbah stopped crying she went over to her, took the girl's hands in her own and said, "Listen to me, Dezbah. You may have many disappointments in your life, but you can't give up."

Dezbah remained silent for quite a while. Shaking herself, she said, "Miss Anderson, you're right. I shouldn't feel sorry for myself. I should be brave like many of my people were when they were faced with the hardships my grandfather tells me about. Let's listen to some music first and then we can do some schoolwork. O.K.?"

"That's my girl! Dezbah, you choose the music. There's enough time today to do both." After the lesson her teacher said, "Dezbah, I would be very pleased if you called me Julie instead of Miss Anderson. You may call me Miss Anderson in front of other people if you wish, but between the two of us I prefer to be called Julie. Can you do me that favor?"

"I like the name Julie. I'll try to remember. I'm not used to calling my teachers by their first names, but this is different. Thanks. Miss Julie," she said, giving her teacher a big grin.

"I have something else to tell you," Miss Julie said, as she prepared to leave. "If your parents will give their permission I would like to take you to a live ballet next Saturday. A traveling ballet company will be in town for the weekend. They are going to do parts of *Swan Lake* and *The Nutcracker* ballets. I know how much you like that music. You'll be able to experience the real thing and see how the dancing and the music work together."

Dezbah's face lit up. "Oh, Miss Julie!" she cried. "What a wonderful surprise! I'll ask my parents if I can go."

Impatient to have her parents return home, Dezbah could not restrain herself when they approached the clearing. "Shimá, shizhe'e, Miss Anderson wants to take me to a ballet performance in town on Saturday. Can I go with her?"

"What will you be doing with Miss Anderson?" her father asked, not understanding what all the excitement was about.

"Miss Anderson has been teaching me about dancing that is different from Navajo dancing. It is called ballet dancing. The dancers will be in town on Saturday. They travel to different places so people can see them. Miss Anderson will come for me."

Dezbah's parents were glad to see their daughter excited about something again. Not since the accident had she been so excited. "If it will make you happy, you can go," her father said, after talking it over with her mother.

Mariana and Jimmy were very glad when they heard what Miss Anderson was doing for Dezbah, but they wanted to do something for her also. They brought her news from school and messages from her friends, but they wanted to so something special. Every day they talked about it.

Several days after Miss Anderson invited Dezbah to the ballet, Mariana said to Jimmy, "Yesterday I saw the cutest puppy someone dropped off at school. I know we have sheep dogs at home, but they are working dogs, not pets. Dezbah has no dog of her own and you know how much she loves animals. What do you think?"

"Great!" shouted her brother. "What a good idea! Dezbah always worries about those homeless puppies. It will make her happy if we rescue one. We can bring it home in a box and surprise her, but we better ask Mom and Dad first!"

That night they told their parents about the puppy. "If you think it will help Dezbah, it's O.K. with us," they said.

The following day Dezbah was sitting by the door of the hogan. Her lessons were over and Miss Julie had left for the day. Once in a while after her teacher left she felt depressed. Today was one of those days. *I'm not in the mood for school talk,* she thought, when she saw her sister and brother approach the clearing. As they drew closer, she noticed that they were carrying a big brown box. *What do they have in there?* she wondered.

Mariana and Jimmy stopped in front of their sister and said in one voice, "Dezbah, close your eyes and open your hands wide!"

The next thing Dezbah felt was a squirmy, furry thing licking her hands. She opened her eyes to see a soft brown puppy with a tiny red tongue hanging out of its wet mouth. She picked up the little animal and peered into its big brown eyes.

"Now you've rescued one of those strays you're always worrying about," Jimmy said.

"Mom and Dad said it's O.K. for you to have it," Mariana added.

"What a wonderful week this has been!" Dezbah exclaimed. "I have a special friend called Julie who

is taking me to a ballet show, and now I have a dog of my very own. I was feeling a little sad before you came home. Thanks for making me feel better."

Holding the pup up for her brother and sister to see, Dezbah said, "Look at her. She's a little furry ball, so furry like a . . . a . . . little bear. Hey, that's what I'll call her, Little Bear — Little Shosh."

"Sister," Mariana said, "some of the girls in your class want to come over Sunday to see you. I told them I'd ask you first if they can come."

"Sure," Dezbah replied. "I'm not going anywhere. It might be fun."

"I'll tell them tomorrow," her sister said.

7

"Oh Shosh, I can hardly wait for Saturday to come," Dezbah said, nuzzling the pup in her arms. Every evening she sat outside the hogan to watch the sunset, holding her furry companion in her lap.

Finally it was Saturday morning and Dezbah's mother helped her bathe and then washed her hair in soap made from the root of a yucca plant. This natural soap gave a lovely luster to Dezbah's long, thick, black hair. For this special occasion her mother put the hair up in a traditional Navajo bun.

Dezbah's mother had been busy sewing all week on her treadle sewing machine. She had said nothing to her daughter about what she was making. When it was time to help Dezbah dress, her mother brought out a beautiful Navajo style blouse and skirt. It was made of light blue cotton

covered all over in a dainty floral print. *What a surprise!* Dezbah's eyes opened wide with delight. "It's so beautiful, shimá! I love it!"

Miss Julie came from town to take Dezbah to the ballet. She wanted to spend the entire day with her pupil and didn't mind driving back and forth the seventy miles each way.

When she arrived at the hogan and took one look at Dezbah, she cried out, "Dezbah, without a doubt you will be the loveliest girl at the ballet!" She could not take her eyes off the excited girl, but it was time to go. She asked Dezbah's father to put her in the car. Jimmy put the wheelchair in the trunk. The entire family stood by the doorway and waved as they drove off.

"Miss Julie, I'm so happy! I can't believe I'm really going to see a ballet. Do you think I'll really like it?" Words kept pouring from Dezbah as they drove along.

Miss Julie laughed. "Dezbah, I have never seen you so excited. It does my heart good. I know you will really like it. Try to calm down and think about the stories and music of the ballet." She started to hum some of the music and Dezbah joined in. The trip went so fast that before they knew it they were at the theater.

All week long Dezbah had been worrying that people would stare at her because she was in a wheelchair, but now she was too excited and happy to feel embarrassed.

Dezbah sat enraptured through the entire performance. *The music, the costumes, the dancing — everything is more than I ever dreamed it would be. If only I had the words to describe my feelings,* she wished.

Miss Julie's eyes were on Dezbah as much as on the stage. She was thrilled by the pleasure the girl was deriving from the ballet. *This has been a memorable afternoon,* she thought.

Miss Julie took Dezbah to a restaurant after the performance. "What did you think of the ballet?" she asked Dezbah after they ordered a light supper.

"I can't seem to find words to describe it," Dezbah answered. "Everything was so beautiful: the dancing, the music, the costumes. It must take a lot of hard work to get so good. I hope I will have a chance to see another ballet."

"I'm so glad you enjoyed it, Dezbah," Miss Julie said. "Now when you listen to your ballet tapes you will get much more pleasure out of them."

They drove home in silence, each immersed in the magical world of ballet. When the car approached the turnoff to the hogan, Dezbah suddenly said, "Miss Julie, if I ever walk again do you think I can become a ballet dancer?" Without waiting for a reply the girl turned forward and was once more in deep thought. Miss Julie's answer was a gentle stroking of Dezbah's luxurious hair.

The next day was Sunday and some of the girls from Dezbah's class came to see her. They found it strange to see Dezbah sitting in her wheelchair. They stood there not saying anything.

"Hi," Dezbah said. "What's happening in the class?"

"Nothing," they said. "Just the same thing every day. What's happening with you, Dezbah? When are you coming back to school?"

"Lots is happening to me," she answered. "Yesterday I went to see a real live ballet show. It was beautiful."

"Like a squaw dance?"

Dezbah shook her head and told them about the performance. They listened politely but said nothing.

"Aren't you bored sitting here all day?" one of the girls asked.

Dezbah told them about Miss Anderson and all the things she was learning; how she was keeping busy reading, listening to music and doing homework.

One of the girls abruptly said, "We have to go. Hope you can come back to school soon."

The girls walked in silence for a while. "What's wrong with Dezbah?" one of them asked. "She sure talks funny."

"Yeah," chimed in another. "She seems so strange. She's different from our 'old' Dezbah."

Later Mariana joined her sister. "How was the visit? They didn't stay very long."

"I told them about the ballet, but they didn't seem to understand." Dezbah shook her head. "Things are so different since my accident. They seemed like strangers to me.

"Maybe when you go back to school everything will be the same as before," Mariana said.

Dezbah was excited when Miss Julie came for her lessons on Monday. The first thing she said was, "My cast is coming off on Wednesday. I won't be here. They say I will be getting crutches in a few weeks to help me walk again, but Miss Julie, I don't want to go back to school. I want you to be my teacher always."

"Things change, Dezbah. Nothing stays the same forever. When the time comes you will be glad to be back in school," Miss Julie said. "I won't be here on Wednesday either. Yesterday, I had a phone call informing me that my mother is sick. She wants me to come to New York to take care of her. I don't think I'll be gone very long. I'll see you as soon as I get back."

Handing Dezbah some papers, Miss Julie continued. "Here's some work for you to do while I'm away. There is no substitute teacher to take my place, but I'm sure Jimmy and Mariana will be glad to work with you when you need help. I'm sorry I can't stay for today's lesson, but I just barely have enough time to get to the airport."

Dezbah put out her good arm to embrace Miss Julie. The young woman responded by giving her a big hug and went quickly to her car. She dared not look back as she drove off.

On Wednesday Dezbah had her cast removed. The doctor asked her father to bring her back in three weeks. "I hope that, by then, her arm will be strong enough to use crutches," he said. "In the meantime, the nurse will give her exercises to do every day to strengthen her arm."

On their next trip to the hospital, Dezbah was given a pair of crutches and shown how to use them. She found them very difficult to manage. "Dezbah, with practice you will be able to use them," the nurse encouraged her. "You must have patience."

The first few days at home Dezbah still had difficulty with the crutches. She had little strength in her arms, particularly the one that had been broken. She was feeling utter frustration. Finally, she gave up in despair. The family pleaded with her to try harder.

"But they hurt. They're clumsy. I can't get used to them," she protested. "I like the wheelchair better."

It was a comfort to her to sit in the wheelchair with her puppy in her lap, listening to beautiful ballet music or reading the books her teacher had left. Her thoughts often went to Miss Julie. *Please come back soon, Miss Julie.* Dezbah kept wishing. *You may be able to tell me why I don't try harder to use my crutches. I am so confused! I have so much I want to say to you. I need your help!*

8

No matter what the weather was like, Dezbah sat outdoors in her wheelchair. Sometimes it was necessary to sit in the doorway of the hogan to protect herself from the rain, the snow or the wind. As time passed she became more aware of the constantly changing landscape of the desert.

When it snowed, the high desert with its buttes and mesas turned into a white fairyland. Lightening often accompanied a rainstorm and Dezbah enjoyed watching it. Looking out on the open sky she saw the jagged flashes of light appear in the west and a moment later appear in the east. This see-saw action often went on for long periods of time. After the storm, a single or double rainbow would arch its way across the vast sky as the sun appeared from behind a cloud.

Shortly after Miss Julie left for New York City, Dezbah's mother said to her, "Grandmother needs my help with the sheep for the next few weeks. I hope you don't mind being by yourself in the afternoon. I'll be here for your lunch most of the time."

"Shimá, I can take care of myself. I don't mind at all. It's more important that you help náali."

"The wind is starting to blow. If it gets too strong, be sure to go inside." With these words of caution, her mother departed taking the younger children with her.

With a sigh Dezbah settled back in the wheelchair to enjoy the quiet afternoon. She loved the desert windstorm. Red sand swirled about tinting the mountains and mesas a misty rose color. The dust from the blowing sand covered the sun, painting the heavens in a magical glow.

The early afternoon wind began to gain strength as the day wore on. Sand was tossed about in the air, whipped into a fury, picking up everything in its path. Dezbah pushed her chair closer to the hogan to protect her face from the stinging sand. She had no intention of going inside despite her mother's warning. She read her book for a while, but soon put it down to watch the show created by the wind.

Looking out on the horizon, Dezbah saw a dust devil spiraling into the air, whipped into a frenzy by the wind. Her eyes followed it for the few moments it took to disappear from view. Many Navajos feared dust devils and would look away, but this one fascinated her. She could not take her eyes away, but she felt safer knowing that it was far off in the distance. She wondered what the attraction was.

"I know!" she cried out. "It reminds me of a ballerina performing a pirouette." Dezbah almost flew out of her chair in the excitement of her discovery. *How graceful it was! If I could only dance like that!* she thought. The helpless girl sank back wearily in her wheelchair.

It was time for Mariana and Jimmy to return from school. She saw them coming down the path and was glad to get her mind on other things. She wished that she could share her experience with them, but she was not sure they would understand how she felt. *If only Miss Julie were here to share it with me,* she thought. *She would understand.*

For the next few days strong winds continued to blow. One afternoon Dezbah sat watching the tumbleweeds tossing about down the path in front of her. They dashed and tangled, whirling on again, pausing and trembling, rolling off into the distance.

The girl, watching them, imagined dancers in crisp beige crinolines, whirling, spinning, bowing, lifting. The vision became so real that she moved her arms in graceful attitudes, and felt her legs tingle and yearn for motion. Dezbah closed her eyes for a moment and saw the dancers of the 'corps de ballet' moving effortlessly on their toes across the stage. Opening her eyes Dezbah gazed once more upon this incredible scene, "They must be dancing just for me!" she called out. "I will call their dance, *The Ballet of the Tumbleweeds.*"

Dezbah wanted to leap from the wheelchair to join in the ballet. But her enthusiasm was cut short when her hands felt her lifeless legs. Her frustration turned to anger!

Why an I still in this wheelchair? Why don't I get down on my hands and knees and join The Ballet of the Tumbleweeds? I must start somewhere if I am going to use my legs again. Isn't that the way babies begin to walk – by first crawling? Dezbah's mind kept spinning around with excitement.

"Come here, Shosh," Dezbah called to her dog. "You and I are going to do this together. We will do it while no one is around. I don't want anyone making fun of me."

Shosh came at Dezbah's call, wagging her tail furiously. The pup stood by while the girl carefully slid out of the chair onto the ground. As she attempted to crawl on her arms and knees she collapsed. Her hands ground into the coarse desert sand, stinging and burning her as she tried to regain her balance. Using all of her strength to steady her arms she was able to move them forward slowly one after the other, but her feet dragged on the ground. Gritting her teeth Dezbah continued in this manner for a few yards.

"I'm going to make it!" she cried out, when suddenly she was hit in the face by a blast of sand tossed about by the wind. The sand got in her eyes making them burn and tear. In a state of panic Dezbah tried to grope her way back to the wheelchair. Shosh sensing something was wrong ran frantically around her.

"Shosh, go!" she yelled, pushing the dog away. She reached for the wheelchair and managed to touch it, but then it rolled out of her grasp. Realizing the wheelchair brake was not set she dragged herself close enough to reach for it. She used all her remaining strength to set the brake, and then with one final effort, hoisted herself into the chair.

Aching all over, Dezbah sat in her chair, disturbed and upset by this new set-back. Not one to cry easily she found herself on the verge of tears. Suddenly annoyed with herself, she said to Shosh, who was now sitting calmly by the chair, "I can't let this stop me. I'm going to try again tomorrow." Seeing how messy she looked Dezbah brushed the sand off her clothes. *I hope no one will notice what happened to me,* she thought.

The next day Dezbah slid out of the wheelchair determined to do better than the day before. Fortunately the wind had calmed down and, learning from the painful experience of the previous day, she remembered to set the brake. She then crawled further than she had before, but she still couldn't get on her knees. Shosh calmly walked alongside her mistress and this time was a comfort to Dezbah.

Dezbah faced each day with more confidence and by the fourth day she was on her knees and felt strong enough to stand. First she stood holding on to a pole in the clearing. Wanting to share her success with someone she patted Shosh on the head. The little dog had faithfully followed alongside her every day, and her presence had given Dezbah encouragement in her struggle to walk. Next, she stood holding onto the wheelchair, moving her legs to and fro. Despite the pain, for the muscles of her legs were weak from disuse, Dezbah gritted her teeth and continued to exercise.

After a few more days of this Dezbah felt confident enough to take a few steps, using the wheelchair for support. She was able to walk a little further each day while holding onto the wheelchair.

Once the strength came back to her legs her old fear left her. After walking around the clearing without using any support she was in a state of ecstasy! *I want Miss Julie to be the first to know of my recovery,* she thought. She took Miss Julie's letter, which she had received several days ago, from her pocket and read it once more:

Dear Dezbah,

It seems so long since I have seen you. I really have missed the pleasant afternoons we spent together. I keep wondering how you are doing. I have good news. My mother is doing fine. I will be seeing you this coming Monday. Say hello to your family.

Love,
Julie

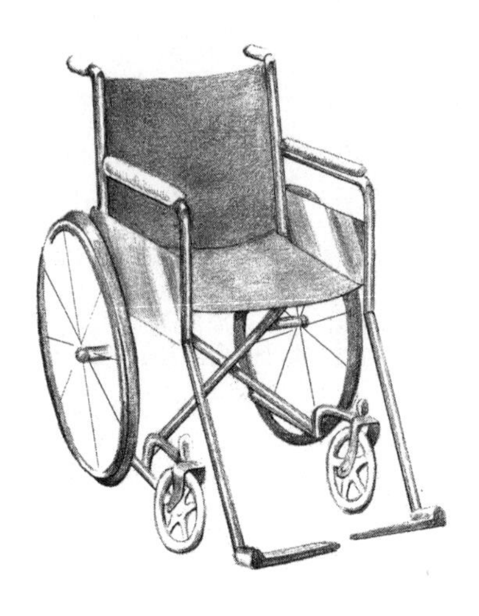

9

The Saturday before Miss Julie was to return from New York City the family was together in the hogan after dinner. Dezbah was becoming anxious to let her family know about her recovery and felt guilty that she had kept the news from them. All was quiet in the hogan when Dezbah blurted out, "Everyone, I have something to show you, but first you must promise not to tell Miss Julie until I do!"

Everyone looked up in surprise. They hadn't seen Dezbah so excited since before the accident. "We promise! What is it? What is it?" they called out at once.

Dezbah stood up, walked over to her mother and embraced her. She then embraced her father followed with hugs for her brothers and sisters.

The questions started to fly.

"How?"

"When?"

"Tell us all about it!"

There was so much happiness in the hogan! Everyone was crying and laughing at the same time.

"Now you won't have to try the crutches again!" shouted Jimmy.

When everyone calmed down Dezbah described what she had seen that led to her walking again. Without mentioning the dust devil she told of the tumbleweeds dancing along the desert path. "It reminded me of the ballet I saw with Miss Julie," she said . . .

"I often think about ballet and wish that someday I may become a ballet dancer. I was so excited watching the performance I named it *The Ballet of the Tumbleweeds.* Right then I decided I had to use my legs again. I remembered that babies first crawl before they walk and that's how I started." She continued telling them the other things she did.

Monday did not come soon enough for Dezbah. She grew impatient as she waited for Miss Julie. It was not yet time for her teacher to arrive, but Dezbah got into the wheelchair which was in its usual place outside the hogan. The anxious girl kept looking at her watch although it was still too early. When Dezbah saw Shosh's tail wagging furiously she knew the dog had heard Miss Julie's car off in the distance. Her heart leaped as she saw it approach.

When the car came to a stop the girl found it almost impossible to remain in the chair. Miss Julie got out of the car with her arms loaded with gifts for the family. Dezbah could wait no longer.

"Miss Julie!" she cried, jumping from the wheelchair and running with outstretched arms.

Miss Julie took one look at Dezbah, dropped her packages and ran to meet her. She embraced the beaming girl. Then, standing back and looking into Dezbah's animated face, she said, "What happened? Why didn't you write to me about this wonderful news?"

"Oh, Miss Julie, I wanted it to be a surprise!"

"And what a surprise it is! You must tell me all about it!" exclaimed the teacher.

"Let's go inside. The sand is blowing too hard," said Dezbah.

Gathering the packages from the ground, Miss Julie said, "Your twelfth birthday was a few weeks ago and I'm sorry I couldn't be here with you. I brought a birthday gift, but getting back the use of your legs is the greatest of all gifts!"

Once inside the hogan and with gifts put away, Miss Julie said, "I can't wait another second. I want to hear all of it!"

"The doctors were right," Dezbah said. "Only my own fears kept me from walking. Thank you for taking me to the ballet. That experience made me want to walk more than anything else."

Dezbah proceeded to tell the entire story, from seeing the first dust devil, to seeing *The Ballet of the Tumbleweeds,* and finally to her struggle to walk.

"What a marvelous tale!" Miss Julie said. "Now you will be going back to school. You do not need my services any longer, but we will certainly continue to be friends."

"If you are sincere about becoming a ballet dancer, I will try to help you reach your goal," continued the teacher. "I will see if there is a dance school in town that you can attend. If there is one you will have to decide soon. It will be more difficult to become a good ballet dancer if you wait until you are older. In fact, most ballet dancers start much younger than you, but because of your running and your determination I think your age won't stand in the way."

Miss Julie then said, "I will have to report to the school that you will be coming in tomorrow. When I'm in your neighborhood I will stop by to see you. When you come to town with your folks please visit me. We can also keep in touch by writing letters. I want to know how you're doing in school."

Miss Julie got up to leave. "I will miss you, Dezbah. I have grown very fond of you. You have taught me many things that are not found in textbooks. Please let me know how . . ."

Before she could finish her sentence Dezbah flung herself into her beloved teacher's arms.

"Oh, Miss Julie, I'll miss you too, but we will see each other again. I'll never forget what you have done for me! Now I can walk you to the car!"

"I'm sorry your folks are not here for me to say good-bye. Tell them I will see them soon," said Miss Julie as the two walked to the car. "Also, tell them how delighted and happy I am that you are walking once more!"

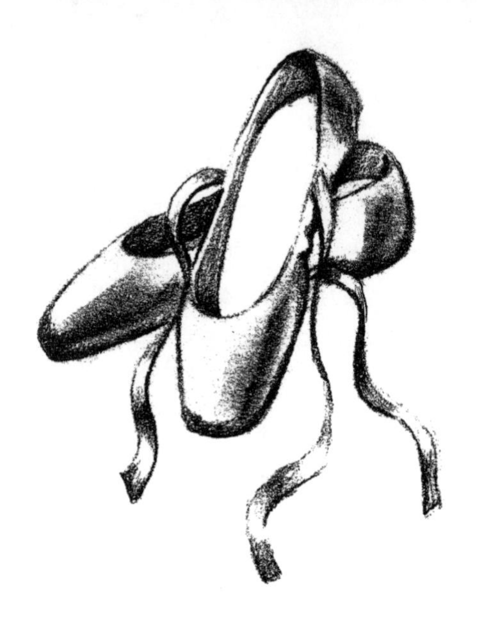

10

Upon her return to school Dezbah was greeted by all her school friends and teachers. "It's good to have you back," everyone said. Dezbah was glad that they didn't ask her any questions about what happened. Now that she knew that it was only her fears which had kept her from walking she didn't like to talk about it.

Dezbah had saved all the papers she had done for Miss Julie, and gave them to her teacher. After looking over the papers her teacher said, "It looks like you have kept up with the class. I'm very pleased."

The experience of the past months gave her a new zest for learning. She became busy with her classroom activities and her grades went way up. She was promoted to seventh grade with honors. She realized that she had Miss Julie to thank for much of her success in school.

Summer vacation had begun, but Dezbah was looking forward to going back to school in the fall. She could hardly wait to be on the junior high track team, but at the same time she thought more and more about ballet dancing.

During the summer Dezbah saw Miss Julie quite often. Whenever Miss Julie was anywhere near Dezbah's home she found time to visit. They talked about music, dancing and books. Also when Dezbah's parents went to town they would drop their daughter off at Miss Julie's house. Despite the difference in age between the two, they had developed a great friendship.

The highlight of the summer vacation for Dezbah was when she attended another traveling ballet performance with Miss Julie. As they were leaving the theater Miss Julie said, "Dezbah, I have good news for you if you're still interested in studying ballet."

"Oh, yes!" replied Dezbah.

"A dance teacher from New York City moved to town and she's opening up a dance studio in September. She teaches all kinds of dance but ballet is her specialty. Most schools give scholarships. When the studio opens I'll ask if she would consider one for you. I'm sure that among your family and friends you can get to town for lessons. You don't have to answer now. Think it over, but let me know soon."

"Will the lessons interfere with my running track in school?" inquired Dezbah. "I still want to become a star runner."

"I don't think it will matter at the beginning. It might even be helpful. Later, you may have to make a decision between running and ballet dancing," Miss Julie answered.

When the dance studio opened in September, Miss Anderson went to see Mrs. Markov, the dance teacher and owner of the studio. She told the woman a little about Dezbah's background and of the girl's desire to become a ballet dancer.

"The problem is that her parents cannot afford to pay for lessons. Do you give scholarships to those who show promise?" Miss Anderson asked.

"Yes," Mrs. Markov answered. "I give several scholarships a year to deserving students who need financial help." She went on to explain what she looked for in a dancer.

"Dezbah has shown me that she is an achiever. She is an inner-directed and self-motivated youngster, needing no prodding. She is also a hard worker," Miss Anderson assured Mrs. Markov.

"Ah, that may be true, but I will have to see for myself," Mrs. Markov said. "Bring her for lessons on the next two Saturdays. Then I will make a decision about a scholarship. There will be no charge for the lessons. You do make her sound interesting!"

Miss Anderson immediately went to see Dezbah and her parents, and repeated her conversation with Mrs. Markov.

"We will find a way to get Dezbah to town if that is what she wants," her parents said.

Dezbah was speechless for a moment but then cried out, "Shizhe'e, shimá, I want to go! Thank you, Miss Julie, for asking."

Saturday morning Dezbah's parents decided to go shopping in town and dropped their daughter off at Miss Julie's house. As soon as Dezbah was inside Miss Julie handed her a package, saying, "Here is a present for you. I hope you will use it for many years."

Dezbah opened the box and was surprised to find a black leotard in her size. "Thanks, Miss Julie."

"Mrs. Markov is lending you ballet shoes for your trial lessons, but if you get the scholarship I'll buy you a pair. Come, it's time to leave for the studio," Miss Julie said.

When Mrs. Markov saw Dezbah walk into the studio she took a quick breath. She could not believe her eyes. The girl had the stature of a classic ballet dancer. Her head was small and her neck long. She had long legs and arms that appeared strong and supple. Every ballet teacher dreams of having a pupil she can develop into a prima ballerina or principal dancer.

Mrs. Markov was very attentive to Dezbah during the entire lesson. When it was over all she said was, "I'll see you next week."

Dezbah and Miss Julie said nothing about the morning. It would be another week before they had an answer and they didn't want to get their hopes up too high.

All that week Dezbah thought about her first lesson. She found it hard to keep her mind on her schoolwork.

"Dezbah, you are not paying attention," her teacher said, when she caught her daydreaming.

"I'm sorry," she said. *I'll be O.K. once I know about the scholarship,* she thought, trying to excuse her inattentiveness.

The following Saturday Dezbah's aunt and uncle took her to the studio where Miss Julie was waiting. Miss Julie sat in the back of the room watching the dancers work at the barre. She kept a close eye on Mrs. Markov. A quiver of excitement went through her when she noticed the pleasure on Mrs. Markov's face as she followed the girl's graceful movements.

At the end of the lesson Mrs. Markov said to Miss Julie, "You were so right. She is a gem in the rough. We will polish her into a fine dancer. I'll see you next Saturday."

Dezbah shyly walked over to the two women and stood there quietly. Mrs. Markov, smiling warmly said, "I'm looking forward to working with you. I believe you have lots of promise."

"Thank you, Mrs. Markov," Dezbah said. "I'll try to do my best."

The two left the studio in high spirits. Miss Julie said, "I'm happy to keep my promise, Dezbah. Let's go to the store to buy your ballet shoes. Afterwards we'll get some ice cream or whatever you want for a treat. We have good reason to celebrate. When your aunt and uncle come we'll have a little party.

There was no problem getting Dezbah to her lessons. There was always someone going to town on Saturdays. When the teachers at school heard of her need for transportation they also volunteered.

Dezbah was eager to work on her dancing during the week, but seven people living in a one-room hogan left no room for warm-up and limbering exercises. Realizing that she would need a place of her own, away from the family and distractions if she were to become a serious and accomplished dancer, she said to her father, "Shizhe'e, I need your help."

"What is it, my daughter? I will help you if I can," he said.

"Shizhe'e, dancing once a week is not enough for me. I must practice at the barre every day but there is no room in the hogan. You know that old shed we don't use anymore? Can we fix it up so I can put up a barre? Mariana and Jimmy said they would help me clean it and patch up the holes. Maybe we can fix the roof so it won't leak when it rains," Dezbah said.

Her father thought for a moment and said, "Yes there's enough old wood around here to fix the roof." In a few days the three children and their father had the old shed fixed. Then her father put up some wooden rods for the barre and laid some spare wood on the floor where Dezbah could work out.

After a few days of practicing, Dezbah realized she needed a mirror behind the barre to watch and study her movements. *I wonder where I can get a long mirror,* she thought. *I know Miss Julie doesn't have one. Maybe I can ask some teachers.* At school the next day she inquired about a mirror but none of the teachers had an extra one.

She decided to enlist the help of Mariana and Jimmy. The next day on the way to school, Dezbah said to them, "I have a problem maybe the three of us can solve. It's important that I have a long mirror behind the barre. I asked some of the teachers and they don't have one. I can't think of anyone else to ask. Think about it during the day and maybe one of you may have an idea. O.K.?"

The two gave their sister a puzzled look. "Where in the world do you think we can get a mirror?"

"In some of the books I've been reading, the heroes always find a solution. Maybe we can," she said.

At the end of the day no one had an answer but Dezbah continued to practice without a mirror. She wouldn't let anything stand in her way of becoming a ballet dancer.

Meanwhile Mariana and Jimmy kept asking everyone they met if they had a mirror they didn't need. Before long everyone in the school heard about the mirror. All the kids on the track team met after school when Dezbah wasn't around and decided to raise the money to buy one. Dezbah was their best runner and they couldn't let her down. Secretly they collected enough money. On Friday the teacher in charge of the junior high lunch period announced to the students that Jimmy had something to say.

Jimmy stood up "I am happy to report we have raised enough money for the mirror." While everyone cheered Jimmy handed the envelope with the money to his sister and said, "Dezbah, the kids on the track team want you to have this money for your mirror."

Dezbah couldn't believe her ears! She got up and thanked her teachers and friends for their generosity. "How happy you have made me! I will work very hard so you will be proud of me some day."

Dezbah kept limber by practicing every day at the barre with the mirror behind it without telling Julie or Mrs. Markov. She wanted to see if Mrs. Markov would notice any big difference in her dancing. After a month of daily workouts Dezbah got her answer.

One Saturday Mrs. Markov said, "Dezbah, what are you doing? Your dancing has improved so much this month, way beyond my expectations. I don't know how you can do it with just one lesson a week!"

Dezbah could not keep her secret any longer. She told her dance teacher how she and her family had converted an old shed into a little dance studio and that she had been working hard at the barre every day for the past month.

"The best part of the story," Dezbah said, "is that the whole junior high school raised money to buy a mirror to put behind the barre. Isn't that great?"

Mrs. Markov turned to Julie, who had accompanied Dezbah to the studio, "You were right. This girl will succeed at whatever she chooses. I hope it will be ballet dancing. Dezbah has everything needed to become an accomplished dancer."

11

Almost four years have passed since I first took Dezbah to Mrs. Markov's dance studio, Julie thought. She was watching the young girl sitting before the mirror, finishing her make-up for the evening's performance.

Everyone had been looking forward to this night. It was the first major public appearance of Mrs. Markov's ballet students. They had given small, intimate recitals for family and a few invited guests, but now it was time for a larger audience. Julie was backstage to wish Dezbah a successful debut.

Dezbah took a final look in the mirror and smiled, pleased with what she saw. It reflected a radiant face, made up to bring out her best features: her almond shaped eyes, firm high cheek bones, and soft but well-shaped lips. The white tutu she

was wearing contrasted with her warm brown skin and shiny black hair done up in a bun atop her head. Dezbah rose from the vanity bench and stretched her willowy arms above her head, then patted a few wisps of hair into place.

She moves with the grace of a swan, Julie thought. *How appropriate it is that she will dance the solo from Swan Lake. She is no longer a little girl, but a most charming sixteen-year old.*

Julie's thoughts continued to wander back to Dezbah's many accomplishments since they met. After overcoming her physical problem Dezbah became the star runner of her junior high track team, breaking records for the 100-meter dash and the 200-meter run. She had graduated from junior high with straight A's and was class valedictorian.

She remembered the day Dezbah had poured out her heart to her. It was shortly after she decided not to run on the high school track team. Julie knew it had been a great sacrifice for Dezbah and had admired the girl for her determination and conviction.

"Julie," Dezbah had said, "I've decided to become a professional dancer. I finally had to choose between running and dancing. I believe I could make it to the Olympics someday and maybe win a medal, but dancing is to be my life's work. Most important is how I feel when I dance. Ballet is probably one of the most aesthetic forms of expression. How do you like that, Julie?" she said, grinning. "I'm picking up lots of new words, aren't I?" Becoming serious again she continued, "It's very thrilling when every part of my body moves to the music. Although it takes lots of hard work, I'm willing to do it."

That was the longest speech I ever heard Dezbah make, reflected Julie, *and I'll never forget it.*

Julie's thoughts were interrupted when Dezbah said, "Thanks for coming backstage to wish me luck, Julie. I'll try my best. I'll be dancing especially for you and my family. Please don't forget to bring your mother backstage when it's over. I've become very fond of her and appreciate her flying all the way from New York City to see me dance. It was a wonderful surprise!"

The bell rang for the dancers to get ready. Julie departed to join her mother and Dezbah's parents out front.

Mrs. Markov had planned a very ambitious program. It consisted of excerpts from Tchaikovsky's *The Sleeping Beauty, Swan Lake* and *The Nutcracker* ballets. Dezbah would be in many of them, but her solo in *Swan Lake* was the most important. Mrs. Markov had chosen dances which would demonstrate her star pupil's ability and talent.

Although Mrs. Markov did not want to lose Dezbah, she knew the girl was ready to study ballet professionally with a top ballet company. Without saying a word to anyone, she had invited an executive member of the Greater New York Ballet Company to see Dezbah perform. It was not often that the ballet company sent someone to a small town, two thousand miles away, to observe an unknown dancer.

Because of Mrs. Markov's excellent reputation as a dance teacher and after quite a bit of urging on her part, the company flew in a 'scout'. The man arrived early that morning and was somewhere in the audience as the curtain went up.

The entire production of Mrs. Markov's dance group was well received by the audience, but the greatest number of curtain calls came after Dezbah's solo performance. People rose to their feet, shouting and clapping, calling Dezbah back time after time.

The elated girl's heart pounded faster and faster each time she returned to the stage to take her bows. Although Dezbah's parents knew little about ballet, the reaction of the audience told them of their daughter's triumph. They joined her backstage with Julie and Mrs. Anderson to share in the celebration of her successful debut.

Meanwhile, the man from New York found Mrs. Markov in the crowd and took her aside. "Mrs. Markov!" he exclaimed. "This has been worth my trip. This girl has a lot of potential. Do you think her parents will let her come to New York? I'm sure we can work out a financial arrangement while she studies with our company."

Mrs. Markov was delighted by the man's response to her star pupil. The two went to Dezbah's dressing room. The dance teacher got everyone's attention when she called out, "I have an important announcement to make. Please listen!" The well-wishers quieted down and all turned toward Mrs. Markov with questioning looks on their faces.

"This is Mr. Petrie, a member of the Greater New York Ballet Company," Mrs. Markov said. "He has something to say to you."

Mr. Petrie repeated what he had said to Mrs. Markov, then proceeded to offer Dezbah a position with one of the greatest ballet companies in the country.

The dressing room was quiet for a moment while everyone tried to absorb what they had just heard.

"Dezbah is young and has never lived in a big city, but she will be well taken care of," he continued. "She will go to high school half the day and work at her dancing the other half. I believe we can develop her into a prima ballerina."

To Dezbah's parents, he said, "I hope you will consider this offer. If there is anything else you would like to know I'll be happy to answer any questions you have."

"Tell us about your dance company," her father requested. "Where will she live and who will see that she comes to no harm?"

Mr. Petrie explained to Dezbah's parents about the arrangements the ballet company would make for her to have a good, safe place to live.

Then he turned to Dezbah, who had been listening attentively, and said, "Dezbah, if your parents give their consent for you to join our company I want to warn you that it won't be easy to become a ballerina. You will be working much harder than you have up until now. There will be times when your feet will hurt so badly and your toes may even bleed. Many dancers drop out as it becomes more difficult. I'm not telling you this to scare you, but to let you know what it takes to become a top ballet dancer."

"Besides, dancing you will be working with all kinds of people, and that may lead to problems. You will get homesick at times. I want you to think about what I've said before deciding," he concluded.

"Thanks, I will," she said to Mr. Petrie as he left the room.

All this time Julie could hardly control her excitement. Now she grabbed Dezbah's hands and exclaimed, "I knew it! I knew it! You will be a great and famous dancer someday. How privileged I was to watch you develop! I hope your parents will let you go to New York. I'll surely go back there more often if they do."

Dezbah, her eyes aglow, hugged Julie. "Thanks for having so much faith in me, Julie. Without your help I would never have gotten this far. I guess I should send a special thanks to those tumbling tumbleweeds, too!" Dezbah laughingly said.

When Dezbah and her parents were leaving, her father said to Mr. Petrie, "What you said sounds good. It is late. Tomorrow we will talk. We'll let you know this week."

Her parents knew it wouldn't be an easy decision to make. The thought of sixteen-year-old Dezbah living so far from home was frightening. Although they had been assured that their daughter would be well taken care of, they knew it was a very big step to make for a young Navajo girl who had never been away from home.

Mariana and Jimmy had remained home to watch the younger children. When the family came home and told them the news they could hardly contain their excitement and pride in their sister.

"Dezbah, you have worked so hard you deserve everything you get." To their parents they said, "Shimá, shizhe'e you should let her go."

Dezbah said nothing. She knew her parents had the final word. Torn between fear of the unknown and joy at the great opportunity that was being offered to her, she was glad they were the ones who would have to decide.

The next day was Sunday. Mariana and Jimmy took the sheep out to pasture while their parents discussed what to do. Her mother was afraid Dezbah would lose her Navajo culture if she went to the big city.

Her father argued that they couldn't stop change. "Life is different than when we were growing up," he said. "Dezbah is different from the other children. We can't stop her from doing what she wants to do. She'll always remember she's a Navajo and not forget her people, no matter where she lives. We have taught her well."

The two could not come to an agreement. The mother suggested that they talk to her parents who lived close by. They left the younger children with Dezbah and departed.

When they arrived at the grandparents' hogan they told the old folks all about the concert and Mr. Petrie's offer to have Dezbah join the ballet company. The parents went on to tell how they felt about Dezbah going off to live in New York City.

Mother worried about her daughter losing her Navajo culture; Father believed that they shouldn't keep Dezbah from doing what she wanted and needed to do. Everyone sat around in silence for some time while each pondered what should be done.

Grandfather finally said, "I agree that Dezbah should go and become a ballet dancer. She shows that she has talent. We have no right to hold her back. She will not forget that she is Navajo. We have taught her to be proud of her people."

Dezbah's grandmother agreed with her husband and then added, "I think Miss Anderson's mother will see that she comes to no harm. If Dezbah is unhappy she can always come home."

"Dezbah is not the same since the accident," her mother said. "You have shown me that I should not stand in her way. We will go home and tell out daughter that she can go with our blessing."

Mariana and Jimmy were back with the sheep when the parents arrived home. The children could hardly wait to hear what they had decided.

Their father remained silent for a few minutes and then with a twinkle in his eye said, "We are going to let Dezbah go to New York."

Mariana grabbed her sister and gave her a big squeeze, then said, "Dezbah, we are so happy for you even though we will miss you. You will be so far away."

"We'll miss you," the other children repeated, nodding their heads and grinning.

Then Father said, "Dezbah, we know how much you want to become a dancer. We will not stop you. Your grandparents say you should go. Your mother is worried that you will lose your Navajo culture, but Grandfather doesn't think so."

"Shimá, I'll never forget," Dezbah reassured her mother. "I've also been thinking about what Mr. Petrie told me and I'm not afraid of hard work. I want to try. I've worked too hard to give up now."

"I am not surprised at your words," her father said. "That is why we are going to let you go. Before you leave we will have a Blessing Ceremony to keep you from harm and to guide your way to success. Now, go to sleep. The last few days have been very hard for you. When you go to school tomorrow you can call Mrs. Markov from the phone booth and give her our answer."

With these words of love and understanding, a new life began for Dezbah.

Glossary of Navajo Words

anglo - white person

bilagáana - a white person

náali - grandmother

shicheii - grandfather or my grandfather

shimá - mother or my mother

shizhe'e - father or my father

sitsoi - granddaughter

yá'át'ééh - hello